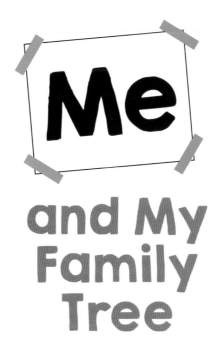

Me
and My
Family
Tree

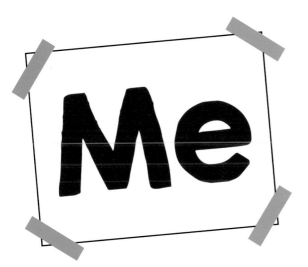

Me and My Family Tree

by Joan Sweeney · illustrated by Emma Trithart

Dragonfly Books ⸺⋇ New York

For Patty, a very special branch of our family tree —J.S.

To every branch of my beautiful family tree —E.T.

Text copyright © 1999 by Joan Sweeney
Cover art and interior illustrations copyright © 2018 by Emma Trithart

Visit us on the Web! rhcbooks.com

Educators and librarians, for a variety of teaching tools, visit us at
RHTeachersLibrarians.com

The Library of Congress has cataloged the previous hardcover edition of this work as follows:
Sweeney, Joan, 1930–2017.
Me and my family tree / by Joan Sweeney ; illustrated by Annette Cable.
1st ed.
New York : Crown Publishers, c1999.
p. cm.
Summary: Using a family tree, a child explains how her brother, parents,
grandparents, aunts, uncles, and cousins are related to her.
[1. Genealogy—Juvenile literature. 2. Families—Juvenile literature. 3.Genealogy.] I. Cable, Annette, ill.
CS15.5 .S94 1999
929/.1 97044201
ISBN 978-1-524-76851-5 (pbk.) — ISBN 978-1-524-76848-5 (trade) — ISBN 978-1-524-76850-8 (ebook)

MANUFACTURED IN CHINA
10 9 8 7 6 5 4 3 2 1
2018 Dragonfly Books Edition

This is me and my family.

I have a brother, a mommy and a daddy, grandparents, aunts and uncles, and cousins too. How are they all related to me? I'll show you on my family tree.

First I start with me.

Then comes my big brother, Alan.

We're both part of my family tree.

These are my parents—Mommy and Daddy.

They're part of my family tree.

This is my mommy's
mommy—my grandma.

This is my mommy's
daddy—my grandpa.

This is my daddy's
mommy—my nana.

This is my daddy's
daddy—my poppa.

They're all part of
my family tree.

Mommy has a sister—my Aunt Sally.
She's married to my Uncle Lee.
They have a daughter—my cousin Alice.

They're all part of my family tree.

Daddy has a brother—my Uncle Jim. He's married to my Aunt Margie. They have two sons—my cousins Jeff and David. Daddy also has a sister—that's my Aunt Pat.

They're *all* part of my family tree. Now—can you guess how I came to be?

Grandma and Grandpa had Mommy and her sister.

Nana and Poppa had Daddy and his brother and sister.

My aunts and uncles had my cousins.

Mommy and Daddy
had my brother.

And then . . .
Mommy and Daddy
had *me*!

One day I may have children, and *they'll* be part of my family tree.

Think of it!
Everyone in
the world has a
family tree.

Just like you and me.